An adaptation
of the animated film
*Raggedy Ann & Andy—
A Musical Adventure*

Target

A TARGET BOOK

published by

the Paperback Division of

W. H. Allen & Co. Ltd

by

KATHLEEN N. DALY

based on the screenplay by

PATRICIA THACKRAY and MAX WILK

A Target Book
Published in 1978
by the Paperback Division of W. H. Allen & Co. Ltd
A Howard & Wyndham Company
44 Hill Street, London W1X 8LB

First published in 1977 in the U.S.A. by
The Bobbs-Merrill Company, Inc.

First published simultaneously in Great Britain in 1978
by W. H. Allen & Co. Ltd and Wyndham Publications Ltd

*Based on the Original Stories and Characters
Created by Johnny Gruelle*

*Raggedy Ann and Raggedy Andy and all related characters
appearing in this book are trademarks of The Bobbs-Merrill
Company, Inc.*

Printed in Great Britain by Hunt Barnard Web Offset,
Aylesbury, Bucks.

ISBN 0 426 20018 7

Contents

Marcella's Playroom

MARCELLA JUMPED off the school bus in even more of a hurry than usual. In one hand she carried her lunch box. In the other she carried a rag doll.

"It's my birthday, my birthday!" she cried happily, giving the rag doll a shake.

She set off at a trot, her feet scuffling through the crisp autumn leaves that lay along the sidewalk and in the gutters. The late afternoon sunlight filtered through the red-gold leaves on the branches and glinted on her long, shining hair.

The rag doll wore a happy smile, even though she *was* being carried by one foot and her head was trailing in the leaves.

Raggedy Ann was always happy, you see, because she had a sweet smile stitched upon her face. And inside her soft, cotton-stuffed body beat a little heart of candy. Anybody who has a candy heart thinks sweet thoughts and spreads love and sunshine all around.

But still, she did wish that Marcella would be a little more careful. Bumpety-bumpety-bump went her head as Marcella bounded up the porch steps.

"Marcella, is that you?" called her mother from the kitchen.

"It's me, it's me!" cried Marcella.

"Hurry up and get ready, dear. It's almost time for your party."

"Yes, Mother," called Marcella.

She flung open the door of her playroom.

"Hello, Susie. Hello, Grandpa. Hello, all you dollies! I hope you haven't been naughty while I've been away."

She climbed up to the bookshelf and picked up a

heavy glass ball. "Hello, Captain, how's your snowstorm today?" As she shook the ball, the "snow" whirled around the little figure of the Captain and his ship.

"Come on, dear," called Marcella's mother.

Marcella put Raggedy Ann gently on a chair.

"Now Raggedy Ann, you take care of all the others while I'm gone," she said.

Then she skipped out of the playroom and closed the door with a slam.

For a moment all was quiet inside the playroom. And then something very strange began to happen. One by one the dolls began to move and sigh and yawn and stretch. Yes, they were coming to life, just as they did every time they were left to themselves, with no real live people around.

"Grandpa, is that door truly closed?" asked Raggedy Ann.

Grandpa Doll trotted over to the door and checked.

"Yes, Annie, the coast is clear, all right."

Raggedy Ann gave a deep sigh.

"Goodness, what a day I've had. Bumpety-bump, bumpety-bump all day. It's always like that when she's excited about something." She felt her head. "I think I must have popped some of my stitches."

"Never mind," said Maxi, trundling over on his wheel. "Maxi will fix your head. Maxi Fix-it, that's me!"

"I'll help you, too," said Susan, the plump Pincushion Doll.

Together they neatened up Raggedy Ann's head.

"There, that's better," said Raggedy Ann. "Thank you."

"The way you go bouncing around with Marcella, it's a wonder you haven't lost all your stuffing," said Susan disapprovingly.

Raggedy Ann laughed. "Oh, but I have. Many's the

time I've come unstuffed and been restuffed and sewn and sewn. I was around long before Marcella, you know. I sat in a box in the attic for fifty years before she found me!"

Nobody could quite imagine what fifty years must be like, so they all stayed quiet for a minute.

"Still, you do get to see the world outside," said Grandpa.

"Yes, the world outside," said the Twin Penny Dolls, who always talked at the same time and said the same things. "Where do you go? What do you see? Do tell! Do tell!"

The dolls never tired of hearing Raggedy Ann tell of the outside world. They gathered around her.

"Well," said Raggedy Ann, "there are so many things—so many beautiful things."

"For instance?" said Maxi.

"There are beautiful butterflies fluttering by. There are leaves, and birds that sing. There are pretty flowers, with bees buzzing around them. And there are lots of people and children and puppies, smiling and happy."

"Is it really like that?" asked Grandpa, holding on to his corncob pipe.

"Yes, it really is," said Raggedy Ann, with her sweet smile.

"Annie, you always make everything seem so beautiful and happy," said Susan.

"Things *are* beautiful," said Raggedy Ann. "But here's the best news of all—it's Marcella's birthday! She's seven years old today."

"Uh—what's a birthday?" asked Barney the Beanbag Doll.

"Well, it's a kind of thing that real live people have every year. They get older, one year at a time."

"And when the year's up, that's your birthday," said Grandpa. "You have parties and fun—and presents! Look over there!"

"*That* certainly looks like a present," said Susan.

"It just came, it just came!" chorused the Twin Dolls.

Raggedy Ann peered hard at the box. What were those strange things sticking out underneath? Oh, but they did look familiar. They looked sort of like her own feet. She stared down at her striped cotton socks and black cotton feet. Then she looked back at the box. Those things looked like—

"Andy!" she screamed. "Is that you?"

The feet wiggled frantically and there was a muffled groan.

HAPPY BIRTHDAY: Marcella
from Paris, France
CONTENTS: one French Doll
xxx Love from Aunt Sophie.

"Oh, dear," said Raggedy Ann. "Poor Andy is under there all squashed. Please, everybody, let's push."

All the dolls gathered around and pushed and heaved. Gradually they got the box over to one side. Raggedy Andy, flat as a pancake, tried to move his wobbly legs.

"Gosh, what a relief!" he said faintly. Everybody helped him up. Susan got busy with her pins.

"Oh, poor Andy," said Raggedy Ann. "I hope it didn't hurt too much."

"Oh, no, not too much," said Raggedy Andy bravely. "Just give me a shake or two and I'll be as right as rain." Like his sister, Raggedy Ann, he could never stay cross for very long.

"Still, it was no fun being under that box all day," muttered Raggedy Andy. "I wonder what's in it."

"There's a label on it, up there, but I can't read it from here," said Raggedy Ann. "Boost me up."

Raggedy Andy, Grandpa, Barney the Beanbag Doll, The Sockworm, Topsy, the Twin Dolls— all the dolls got together in an untidy heap. There was so much giggling and heaving that the heap kept falling apart, but at last Raggedy Ann made her way to the top and grabbed the label.

"It says, 'Happy Birthday, Marcella, from Paris.

Contents: One French Doll. Love from Aunt Sophie.' "

"Ooh!" gasped the Twin Dolls. "Imagine that!"

"A doll all the way from Paris!" exclaimed Maxi.

"Another doll," groaned Raggedy Andy, quite unlike his usual cheery self. Marcella would have been surprised to see that his mouth was pulled down at the corners. "That's all we need—another doll. A *girl* doll, all sugar and spice, I bet."

"Andrew, you're just terrible," said Raggedy Ann. "It must be because of being squashed all day."

"Anyone would feel the same," said Grandpa sympathetically. "Who wants to be squashed all day—even by a French doll?"

Maxi grinned. "I wouldn't mind."

Suddenly Grandpa was waving his arms up and down. "Freeze!" he said. "Here comes Marcella!"

Quickly the dolls hurried back to where Marcella had left them. All except Raggedy Andy, who flopped down just beside the box, smiling sweetly.

The
French Doll

THE DOOR to the playroom flew open, and in came Marcella. Her cheeks were flushed and rosy. She wore a silver paper crown.

"Oh, Raggedies, what a lovely party I'm having! But I couldn't wait one more minute to come up and see my surprise. It's from Paris!"

She slipped the string off the box and ripped open the brown paper. There were oceans of pink tissue paper, crinkling and rustling. Finally Marcella pulled out a doll. But this was no ordinary doll.

"Ooh!" gasped Marcella. "A French doll!"

The doll was very beautiful. She had painted cheeks and a little rosebud mouth. Her hair was blond and tightly curled. Her eyes were shiny blue, fringed with long, dark eyelashes.

Marcella stroked the soft hair and smoothed out the long skirt and petticoats.

"What shall I call you?" she wondered aloud. She tipped up the doll to look at the pretty white underwear.

"Ba-bette . . . Ba-bette," said the doll's little mechanical voice.

"Babette," breathed Marcella. "How lovely. Look, dollies, here is a new friend for you. Look, Raggedy Ann, isn't she the most gorgeous, beautiful doll you ever saw in your whole life?"

Raggedy Ann smiled sweetly.

"You poor dear," said Marcella to Babette. "You've had such a long trip, all the way from Paris. You must be tired. I'm going to put you to bed in the doll's-house."

The doll's-house was very quaint and old-fashioned. It had been in Marcella's family for many years. It had a slanting roof and dormer windows. There were blue shutters that opened and closed.

Marcella opened up the hinged roof.

"This will be your house, Babette," said Marcella.

She put Babette in the biggest bedroom.

"Marcella! Come on down and blow out your birthday candles!"

"Coming, Mother," Marcella called downstairs. "Now, Babette, you settle down and rest. And you, Raggedy Ann, *dear* Raggedy Ann, make sure that Babette feels right at home every minute. She's a stranger here, and you and all the other dolls must be especially nice to her. See you soon!"

Marcella blew them all an airy kiss and skidded out the playroom door, which closed with a bang.

There was a moment's silence while the dolls made sure that Marcella was on her way.

Raggedy Ann was the first to stir. She untwined her legs and walked over to the doll's-house.

"Welcome to the playroom, Babette," she said softly.

There was no answer from the doll's-house.

"Babette?"

Raggedy Ann knocked on the door.

Raggedy Andy gave it a big thump, cupped his hands, and yelled, "Babette!"

The little blue door on the balcony opened and Babette came out, blinking sleepily.

"What is it? Who are you? What is this place?"

"My name is Raggedy Ann," beamed the little doll. "And this is my raggedy brother, Andy. Welcome, Babette!"

Babette blinked again, so that the long eyelashes fluttered.

"But where am I?" she asked.

"You're in the playroom, that's where," said Raggedy Andy. "Lots of dressing up and tea parties and things like that—*you'll* probably love it." He rubbed his elbow that was still a little out of shape from having been squashed all day.

Raggedy Ann gave him a look from one of her bright shoe-button eyes. "Now, Andy, we're supposed to be nice and make her feel welcome, remember?"

"Oh, dear," said Babette, "I have never been in a place like this. I come from the most expensive toyshop in Paris. You all look so—different."

"Never mind," said Raggedy Ann kindly. "You'll love it here with us."

"But—what exactly are you?" asked Babette. "I have never seen things like you before. In the toyshop, all the dolls had beautiful clothes and shiny faces and curly hair . . ."

"We are dolls, too," said Raggedy Ann. "Each of us is different on the outside. Some fat, some thin, some floppy, like Andy and me. But, you know, Babette, it doesn't matter what you look like outside, so long as you are beautiful inside."

Captain
Contagious

SUDDENLY there was a loud "A-choo!"

It was the Captain in the glass ball. He felt a little out of things, up there on the bookshelf.

"What's going on?" he asked his parrot Queasy. "Can't see a thing in here with all this blasted snow. Bring me my spyglass."

Babette didn't even hear him. She shook her head sadly. "I don't understand," she said. "This is so different from Paris. I wish I were home again."

"But this is your home now," said Raggedy Andy. "Why, Raggedy Ann is the sweetest, kindest doll in all the world. She will love you with all her loving candy heart. And so will we all—you wait and see."

Babette sighed and shook her head. Just as the Captain focused his spyglass upon her, a tiny, starry tear trickled from one blue eye.

"Shiver my timbers," said the Captain, his moustaches twirling. "What a beautiful doll! She's like a dream come true. I think she is my one and only true love, finally come right here to the playroom!"

Babette didn't hear him. She sighed again and turned to go into the house.

"I think she's a little homesick," said Raggedy Ann. "Poor thing. Perhaps she'll feel better after a good night's sleep."

The little blue door closed behind Babette.

"Queasy," yelled the Captain, "we must get out of here. A-a-choo!"

"Aye, aye, Captain," squawked the parrot. He had his eye on the Cuckoo Clock. It hung on the wall right near the Captain's shelf. And the hands of the clock were just moving up to the hour—five o'clock.

Quickly Queasy scratched the letters SOS, which meant HELP! on the glass inside the ball. The Captain's long whiskers curled around the letters.

At exactly five o'clock the yellow wooden doors of the Cuckoo Clock sprang open.

"Cuckoo-cuckoo-cuckoo-cuckoo-cuckoo!" screamed the Cuckoo. He knew his job all right, and he was proud of it. One "cuckoo" for every hour of the day.

On the fifth "cuckoo" he suddenly noticed the Captain, waving wildly. He saw the message scribbled on the glass wall.

"Oh," he said, which is very unusual for a Cuckoo Clock.

All the dolls looked up in amazement.

The Cuckoo came zooming down on his spring. He grabbed Raggedy Ann's yarn hair in his beak and sprang back, and Raggedy Ann landed on the shelf beside the glass ball.

"What is it? What's the matter?" asked Raggedy Ann.

Then she saw the Captain jumping up and down in clouds of snow. She saw the HELP message scribbled on the glass.

"Oh, my goodness," she said. "The Captain needs help. I'll do my best, Captain," she said. "Put me down please, Cuckoo."

The Cuckoo dropped her as gently as he could, and Raggedy Ann landed with a *plop* on the playroom floor.

"Are you all right? Are you all right?" asked the Twin Dolls.

"Oh, yes," said Raggedy Ann, smiling. "We Raggedies don't have anything to break, you know. It's the Captain who needs our help. I think he wants to get out."

They all gazed up at the Captain, who was prancing up

and down, his long moustaches twirling, yelling things that they couldn't hear.

"You're right," said Raggedy Andy. "What are we going to do?"

"I must think," said Raggedy Ann.

She sat down in a heap and pulled her rag face down into a frown. Thinking was always difficult.

"Be careful, dear," said Susan, ready with her pins. Thinking always made Raggedy Ann's stitches come loose.

"I know!" said Raggedy Ann. "Maxi, look in your tool-box. Maybe you have a tool that can cut glass."

"I'll look," said Maxi. He took off his hat and felt inside his head. "Aha—the very thing!"

He drew out a very sharp-looking tool. "It's a glass cutter—for cutting glass," he said proudly.

"Oh, you are wonderful, Maxi," said Raggedy Ann. "Let's try it. Up, please, Mister Cuckoo Bird."

The Cuckoo hadn't had so much fun in years. He zoomed down again and grabbed Raggedy Ann's yarn hair. Maxi clung to her waist, and up they went.

"Now stand back, please," said Maxi.

Carefully he cut a circle in the glass. He tapped it gently with a hammer.

Suddenly a perfect circle of glass fell out of the ball.

"Look out!" yelled Maxi.

Nobody expected what happened next.

Kidnapped!

WATER CAME gushing out of the hole, and with it came the Captain, his ship, his spyglass, and Queasy, squawking loudly for all to hear.

Everyone got very wet indeed, all except the Cuckoo. He sprang hastily back into the safety of his clock.

"Free at last!" cried the Captain. "Now I can claim that beautiful doll!"

Sea water sloshed over the playroom floor. All the dolls found themselves floating and gasping in the salty water. Most surprising of all, the Captain's ship got bigger and bigger.

"Avast! Belay!" He yelled all the nautical words he knew, and some of them were very naughty. His ship, which had been so tiny in its glass ball, was suddenly a splendid three-masted galleon, with a full crew of sailors. In fact, they were not only sailors, they were Pirates, with long black whiskers and striped jerseys, and each had a patch over one eye. They wore boots and carried wicked-looking cutlasses.

"Dear me, Captain," said Raggedy Ann, who was floating face up in the salty water. "What on earth are you doing?"

"Lay back there, Missy!" yelled the Captain. "I have come to claim my prize!"

"What prize?" gurgled Raggedy Andy, hoping desperately that his cotton stuffing wouldn't get soaked and send him to the bottom.

"My treasure! The beautiful Babette! A-choo!"

"Oh, dear," said Raggedy Ann, "I'm afraid you're going to catch a cold instead."

"Queasy, dowse the lights!" yelled the Captain.

Queasy flew up to the light and pulled the string. Suddenly there was darkness in the playroom.

The Captain made a rope out of his long whiskers and climbed up to Babette's balcony. A door smashed open. Babette shrieked. Then, kicking and screaming, she was carried out by the Captain. He brought her aboard his ship while the Pirates sang, "Yo ho for the life of a Pirate!"

"They are very naughty indeed," sighed Raggedy Ann, her little candy heart beating fast. "I don't know what's to become of them."

"Pull, me hearties!" cried the Captain. "Away we go!"

And away they went, the Pirates pulling lustily upon their oars, across the playroom floor, out the window, and into the night.

"Oh, how naughty," said Raggedy Ann. Still, she couldn't help admiring the song of the wicked Pirates as it faded into the distance.

"Yo ho, yo ho for the life of a Pirate!" they sang. "Trim the mizzen and shiver the timbers and hoist the main, yo ho!"

"The life of a Pirate is the only life for me!" joined in the Captain.

"*Eeeeek!*" screamed Babette.

"It's all my fault," said Raggedy Ann. "I should never have let him out."

The salty water had all disappeared with the wicked Captain and his crew. The dolls were shaking themselves and spluttering.

"Andy, I've got to save Babette!" said Raggedy Ann.

"You're not going after her?" said Grandpa, feeling slightly stiff after his soaking.

"Not into the Deep Deep Woods!" said Susan.

"It's really scary, really scary in the Deep Deep Woods," said the Twin Dolls, holding on to each other.

"I don't care how scary it is," said Raggedy Ann. "I've got to get Babette back for Marcella. It's her birthday doll."

"You're right," said Raggedy Andy. "I'm coming with you. After all, somebody's got to protect you."

The two Raggedies walked over to the windowsill and climbed up.

Raggedy Ann stood on the windowsill and looked down at all the little faces. "Now you stay here and wait. We'll be back before morning—just wait and see."

"And Marcella won't even know anything happened," added Raggedy Andy, sounding much braver than he felt. "I'll go first." He peered down into the darkness.

"No, I will," said Raggedy Ann. "It was all my fault."

"Ooh, ooh!" gasped the Twin Dolls as Raggedy Ann dropped out of the window.

"Now me," said Raggedy Andy. He gave a couple of little jumps to give himself courage. Before he knew it he was over the edge.

"Are you all right, Annie?" he gasped, trying to untangle his feet.

He helped Raggedy Ann up.

"I'm all right—I think," said Raggedy Ann. "How about you, Andy?"

"Oh, sure, of course," said Raggedy Andy.

They straightened themselves out, holding on to each other. The window of the playroom seemed awfully far above them. Ahead loomed the dark shadows of the Deep Deep Woods.

Where anything can happen.

The Camel
with the
Wrinkled Knees

"ARE YOU afraid, Andy?" asked Raggedy Ann.

"Me, scared?" said Raggedy Andy. "Why should I be scared?"

"It is a *little* scary," said Raggedy Ann. "Ooh—what's that?"

"It's only an old hoot owl," said Raggedy Andy, clutching Raggedy Ann tightly. "Don't be afraid. I'll take care of you."

"You are brave, Andy," said Raggedy Ann.

"It's easy to be brave when we're together," said Raggedy Andy. "Besides, I've got this paper daisy you gave me once, the time I got washed and starched by mistake, remember?"

Raggedy Ann giggled. "Yes, and you were too stiff to move for weeks."

"Well, your paper flower cheered me up, and I've been carrying it around ever since."

"Oh, Andy, it's great that we've got each other."

Suddenly Raggedy Ann stopped and held her breath. "What's that, Andy?" she whispered.

"What's what?" said Raggedy Andy.

A funny whistling sound came from the darkness of the Deep Deep Woods.

"Oh, that," said Raggedy Andy. His raggedy knees were shaking just the tiniest little bit, but he put a firm arm around Raggedy Ann's shoulders.

"Don't worry, Annie. Whatever it is, I'll protect you."

Sigh, groan, snuffle . . . the sounds were coming nearer.

"Here it comes," whispered Raggedy Ann. The bushes ahead of them rustled, and a large head poked out.

"Come on out, whoever you are," said Raggedy Andy.

The head looked at them for a moment. Then out came the rest of the creature. It was a camel. But such a camel as you never saw in any zoo. He was made of soft woollen cloth and stuffed with sawdust. At one time he may have been a very handsome, important-looking camel. But he had been played with so much that now he had lumps where no self-respecting camel is supposed to have lumps. And his legs, instead of being straight and stiff, were all wrinkly and baggy at the knees. When he moved, it seemed as if he would trip over at every step. And he was *blue*.

Raggedy Andy took one astonished look, then leaped forward and flung his arms around the Camel's neck.

"Got you!" he cried bravely.

The Camel's knees sagged more than ever, and he fell in a crumpled heap, giving a great, squashy kind of groan.

"Andy, he's just a poor old camel," said Raggedy Ann, rushing forward. "Let him go!"

"Oh, dearie me," groaned the Camel with the Wrinkled Knees. "I'm afraid my legs aren't quite what they used to be. Once they had good, straight sticks inside them. You should have seen me then."

"Oh, poor, dear Camel," said Raggedy Ann. "Here, let me help you up."

The Camel with the Wrinkled Knees

Together Raggedy Ann and Raggedy Andy heaved and pushed. At last the Camel with the Wrinkled Knees was standing almost upright.

"Thank you, thank you, much obliged," he said. He lifted his long, wrinkled neck and gazed up into the sky. "It's too bad you tripped me up. Now they have gone," he said.

"Gone?" said Raggedy Andy. "Who have gone?"

"Those lovely camels in the sky—a whole caravan of them, with nice straight legs and graceful necks, and all looking so happy and smiling . . ."

"Are you *sure?*" asked Raggedy Ann. She and Raggedy Andy were both staring up at the sky, but all they could see were the stars twinkling through the branches of the trees.

"Oh, yes," sighed the Camel with the Wrinkled Knees. "I often see them. I've been chasing them for ages. If only I could catch up with them, think how happy I'd be. I wouldn't be sad and alone any more. I'd have friends who

would love me. They'd smooth out all my wrinkles, and I wouldn't be low-down saggy and raggy-baggy blue." He heaved such a deep sigh that Raggedy Ann was afraid he would fall over again.

"Oh, poor, dear Camel," she said, holding him up with her little shoulder. "Please, please, don't be sad. Andy and I will be your friends, won't we, Andy?"

"Oh, yes," said Raggedy Andy. "We'll be really-truly friends, and you'll see—everything will get better. Why, Annie here has the kindest heart in the world. It's a sugar-candy heart and it says on it, 'I love you.' *Everyone* is happy when Annie is around."

"My," said the Camel with the Wrinkled Knees, "that *does* sound nice. To have real friends. Are you sure?"

"Of course we're sure," said Raggedy Ann and Raggedy Andy together.

Suddenly the Camel with the Wrinkled Knees sagged again. Raggedy Ann and Raggedy Andy heaved him up.

"I can never be sure of anything," he moaned. "That's why I'm always chasing those camels in the sky. Look, look, there they are again!"

He started to move forward, sagging and swaying. "Quickly, come with me, or we'll lose them again!"

Raggedy Ann and Raggedy Andy looked up at the blue night sky. Then they looked at each other.

"I don't see anything, Andy, do you?"

"No," whispered Raggedy Andy. "This is really weird. Look at him go! We'd better hop aboard."

Nimbly they sprang on to the Camel's back, holding on very tight as the lumpy creature sagged and swayed, going faster and faster, his eyes on the sky.

"Mister Camel, please slow down," begged Raggedy Ann. "There are no camels up there!"

"There's happiness up there," said the Camel with the Wrinkled Knees. "I've been looking for happiness all my life. Can't let it get away from me now."

"Whoa, whoa!" yelled Raggedy Andy.

They were starting to climb a very steep hillside.

"Please be careful!" cried Raggedy Ann. "We're going too fast, and we don't know what's on the other side of the hill. Oh, please, Mister Camel . . ."

But it was too late. They had reached the top of the hill and had gone clean over the edge. They were falling through the air, arms and legs flying, going down, down . . .

The
Greedy

THE THREE—Raggedy Ann, Raggedy Andy, and the Camel with the Wrinkled Knees—slid down a slippery slope, their arms and legs all tangled up together.

They came to a slurpy, slithery, gooey stop at the bottom.

The Camel with the Wrinkled Knees groaned.

But Raggedy Andy, smelling something familiar, put out his hand and took up a dab of the sticky stuff.

He tasted it.

"It's toffee!" he said. "Really delicious toffee. Taste it, Annie."

"Yum," said Raggedy Ann. "It's almost as good as that toffee we made one night in the kitchen back home; do you remember, Andy?"

"Oh, yes," said Raggedy Andy. "What a lovely mess we made!"

"But we *did* clean it up," said Raggedy Ann. "It looks to me as if no one has done any cleaning up around here for a long time. Look at that—a giant cherry."

She reached over to pull the cherry out of the sea of toffee—and it started to move!

In fact, it started to grow.

In fact, "it" was alive.

"Urp," it gurgled. "Oh, excuse me. Pardon me. Who are you?" It looked at the two little dolls and the Camel with the Wrinkled Knees, who was sagging more than ever in the sweet, sticky stuff.

"Who are *you*?" said Raggedy Andy.

"I am the Greedy. And this is the Toffee Pit. Welcome to my home."

"What sort of a place is this?" asked Raggedy Andy, as a chocolate cupcake went sailing by.

"It's the sweetest place in the world," said the Greedy, rolling his eyes. "I've gathered sweets—every kind of sweet you ever thought of—from all over the place. They are all here. But I can never get enough to eat. Never, ever."

"Oh, dear," said Raggedy Ann. "That's terrible. Is there anything we can do to help?"

"Yes," burped the Greedy. "Excuse me. If you could only tell me where to find a sweetheart . . ."

"A *what*?" asked the Camel with the Wrinkled Knees, struggling on to his wrinkly knees.

"A sweetheart," said the Greedy. "I'm not sure exactly what it means, but an old Chinese fortune cookie told me I would find happiness and never be hungry again if I could only find a sweetheart."

"You have all this stuff around you, and you need a sweetheart as well?" gasped Raggedy Andy.

"Yes," said the Greedy sadly. "I've got everything—candyfloss, chocolate bars and lollipops, ice cream and fudge sauce, butterscotch and nuts to make your mouth water. But—"

"But what?" asked the Camel with the Wrinkled Knees.

"But without a sweetheart, it's no use. It's never enough."

"Oh, dear me," said Raggedy Ann. "I'm really very sorry for you."

"Yes," gurgled the Greedy. "It's a sad case, all right. I've got fruitcake, sugar icing, honey dribbling down my chin. I've got cream puffs and crunchy almonds, but it's just no good."

"Some people are never satisfied," muttered Raggedy Andy, who was beginning to feel a little sick.

"Squash me a banana drowned in jelly, tutti-frutti by the score, marzipan and pastry, caramel and gingerbread galore—none of it's any good, because I have no sweetheart."

"Poor old Greedy," said Raggedy Ann. "That's a very sad story. By the way, my name is Raggedy Ann, and this is my brother, Raggedy Andy, and that is the Camel—"

"—with the Wrinkled Knees," added the Camel, on his feet at last.

"How do you do?" burped the Greedy.

"We fell into your Toffee Pit by mistake. But now we must be on our way," said Raggedy Ann.

"Why do you have to leave so soon?" asked the Greedy.

"We have to rescue a friend," said Raggedy Ann.

"From Pirates," said Raggedy Andy. He tried to shift his feet, but they seemed to be stuck fast in the gooey toffee. "Would you please let us go, Mister Greedy?"

"Oh, no, please don't go," said the Greedy. "Please help me find a sweetheart. You have no idea how miserable life can be when you are surrounded entirely by peanut-butter custard and baked Alaska—and no sweetheart."

"I'm sorry, Mister Greedy. I'd really like to help you, but I'm only a little rag doll with a little candy heart, and . . ."

"What did you say?" gulped the Greedy.

"I said I'd like to help you, but I'm only a rag doll . . ."

"With a candy heart?" said the Greedy.

Raggedy Ann nodded.

"If it's a candy heart it must be sweet," said the Greedy, licking his lips. "A real sweetheart."

"I suppose it must be," said Raggedy Ann.

"Well, then, I'd like to have it," said the Greedy.

"It seems to me, Mister Greedy, that you've got quite enough already," said Raggedy Ann, backing away.

"But I told you—it's never enough until I have a sweetheart, and at last I've found one."

"Don't touch one little stitch of that little dolly," said Raggedy Andy.

"Simmer down, sonny," said the Greedy. He plopped a glob of cream on Raggedy Andy's head.

"Don't treat Andy like that!" said the Camel with the Wrinkled Knees, straightening up for a minute.

"I'll treat anyone the way I like," said the Greedy. "It's my Toffee Pit, and I'm going to have that sweetheart for my very own."

He produced a pair of scissors from a sticky pocket in his toffee suit.

"Don't you go near that little rag doll!" said the Camel with the Wrinkled Knees.

"Oh, please, Mister Greedy, don't take my candy heart," said Raggedy Ann. She started to run, slipping and sinking into the toffee. *Snip-snap* came the sound of the scissors close behind her.

"You big bully," yelled the Camel with the Wrinkled Knees. He charged, head first, into the Greedy. His head disappeared right into the Greedy's pudding of a body.

The Greedy kept on after Raggedy Ann, who was trying to run. Her feet kept sinking down into the treacly stuff. It was hard to move. Poor Raggedy Ann! She really didn't want to lose her little candy heart. She remembered how, long ago, she had fallen into a paint bucket. The painter's nice mother had washed Raggedy Ann and completely restuffed her with nice clean stuffing. Before she stitched Raggedy Ann up, she had sewn in a little candy heart that said on it, "I love you." That was why Raggedy Ann really did love everybody and always wanted to help.

But she was sure she wasn't meant to give up her candy heart to the Greedy.

"Don't worry, Annie," said Raggedy Andy. He was throwing ice-cream snowballs into the Greedy's eyes.

"Stop, stop, I can't see where I'm going!" cried the Greedy.

"Come on, let's run," cried Raggedy Andy. "Camel, get your wrinkled knees out of there."

The Camel with the Wrinkled Knees came out from the Greedy's pudding of a body. "My, that was delicious," he said.

The three ran and stumbled and slithered and slid toward the walls of the Toffee Pit.

"Come back here!" yelled the Greedy. He had a great big pastry tube and was firing vanilla ice cream at them.

"Oh, it's so good," groaned Raggedy Andy.

"Don't give in," said Raggedy Ann. "We've got to keep going."

They were trying to climb the walls of the pit, but there was nothing for them to hang on to. They kept sliding back down to the bottom.

"That's right, come on down, sweetheart," crooned the Greedy.

"Take that!" cried Raggedy Andy. He jumped on to a jam doughnut, and the red jam squirted into Greedy's face.

"Yum! You throw good stuff," said the Greedy.

Then he started to throw striped candy canes at them. The sticks hit the wall—*thump, thump, thump.*

"A staircase!" cried Raggedy Ann. "Look, now we've got something to hold on to."

Dragging the sagging Camel with the Wrinkled Knees between them, Raggedy Ann and Raggedy Andy slowly climbed the candy-cane ladder, pulling out each cane as they came to it and placing it one notch higher.

"I'll never make it," groaned the Camel with the Wrinkled Knees. "You kids go on without me."

"Never!" said Raggedy Ann. "You're coming with us."

"You can make it," said Raggedy Andy. "Please, please try."

They arrived at a ledge halfway up the wall. With a final heave they managed to get all four of the Camel's legs up. He flopped down with a mighty sigh.

"Look," said Raggedy Andy, "a marshmallow boulder! Come and help me move it over the edge."

Together the three of them pushed and struggled. The boulder began to move. Slowly they rolled it toward the edge, and over it went.

"Hurray!" they shouted.

Down went the marshmallow, picking up speed as it went. Gumdrops and chocolate candies stuck to its sides. It rolled through a patch of raspberry jam. It got bigger by the minute—and it was heading straight for the Greedy.

"Help, help!" he cried. But he was too fat to ooze out of the way in time. The marshmallow hit him right in the face. "Ooh," he groaned, "how delicious! That's a *new* flavour. Oh, yum!"

"Come on, let's go," said Raggedy Andy.

"I do hope he finds a real sweetheart someday," said Raggedy Ann kindly.

The
Loonie Knight

RAGGEDY ANDY PULLED and Raggedy Ann pushed, and at last they got the Camel with the Wrinkled Knees over the top of the cliff.

"My, it's good to be back in the Deep Deep Woods," said Raggedy Ann.

The moonlight was streaming down through the leaves, making ribbons of light amongst the mysterious blue-green shadows. The great trees moved their branches in the gentle breeze, and the leaves whispered to each other.

"Ooof," panted the Camel with the Wrinkled Knees. "May we sit down and rest a little?"

"Yes, let's," said Raggedy Andy.

The three of them flopped down under a tree.

"What an adventure," said Raggedy Ann. "Thank you both for saving me."

"That's what friends are for," said the Camel with the Wrinkled Knees.

"That's right," said Raggedy Andy. "And when we take you home with us, you'll meet lots more friends."

Suddenly the Camel with the Wrinkled Knees stumbled to his feet.

"Listen, there they are again—those beautiful camels in the sky."

"No, no, Mister Camel," said Raggedy Ann.

The two Raggedies held on tightly to the Camel with the Wrinkled Knees.

"You were only dreaming again," said Raggedy Andy. "Come on, we must find Babette before morning. The sooner we all get back to Marcella's playroom, the better."

Raggedy Ann nodded, looking anxiously at the Camel with the Wrinkled Knees.

"Who is Babette? Who is Marcella?" asked the Camel with the Wrinkled Knees, still looking up at the sky, with his eyes going around in circles.

"Babette is a beautiful French doll, and Marcella is a little girl," explained Raggedy Ann.

"Marcella is *home*," said Raggedy Andy. "We all live in Marcella's playroom. But some wicked Pirates stole Babette away. We must find her and bring her back—"

"—or Marcella will be very sad," finished Raggedy Ann.

None of them noticed a pair of large eyes gazing at them through the bushes.

"We're going to do our very best to find Babette before morning," said Raggedy Andy, getting to his feet. "Come on."

The eyes in the bushes rolled. A grinning face appeared, and then some crooked legs. In between, there seemed to be a large tin can.

"Stick 'em up!" said the creature, holding out a gun.

"BANG!" went the gun, and out came a flag that said, YOU NEED HELP!

"You need help!" screeched the tinny-looking man,

laughing wildly. "I bet you want to know where Babette is—am I right?"

"Yes! How did you know that?" gasped Raggedy Ann.

"And who are you, anyway?" asked Raggedy Andy.

"I'm Sir Leonard, the Looniest Knight in the Year," said the tin can, rattling with mirth.

"How do you do?" said Raggedy Ann politely.

"Haw haw haw!" boomed the Loonie Knight.

"I don't see what's so funny," said Raggedy Ann.

"Well, maybe this will help you to see," said the Loonie Knight.

He held a telescope over Raggedy Ann's eye.

"I don't see *anything*," said Raggedy Ann. She took away the telescope, and the Loonie Knight doubled up with laughter.

Raggedy Ann had a black circle around her eye where the telescope had been.

"Hee hee hee, you've got a black eye!" shrieked the Loonie Knight.

"You lay off my sister, Sir Leonard," said Raggedy Andy angrily.

"What's wrong with a little fun?" said the Loonie Knight.

"Fun at the expense of others isn't nice," said Ann.

"Oh, that's *very* funny," giggled the Loonie Knight.

"Stop this craziness," said Raggedy Andy. "We must go and find Babette."

"Of course you must," said the Loonie Knight. "And I'm the very person to help you. Here, have some gum."

Raggedy Andy took the stick of gum, and it snapped on his finger like a mousetrap.

"Ouch!" yelled Raggedy Andy.

"Ho ho ho," laughed the Loonie Knight. "Welcome to Loonieland." He took a banana from his tin-can suit and began peeling it. "Loonieland is where all the practical jokes in the world come from. And guess what? We're going to try them all out on *you*!"

"Come on, let's get out of here," said Raggedy Andy.

He grabbed Raggedy Ann by the hand, and the three of them started to run.

The Loonie Knight threw his banana peel just ahead of Raggedy Andy. And of course Raggedy Andy slipped on it and flopped down.

"Beautiful!" shrieked the Loonie Knight. "I love it! You're in Loonieland; and now that you're in, you'll never get out!"

Raggedy Ann helped Raggedy Andy to his feet. The two little dolls tried to smile, but inside they were not very happy.

"That was a mean thing to do," said Raggedy Ann. "Why are you doing all this to us?"

"For laughs, of course," said the Loonie Knight. "I love you because you are such dear little dollies—you don't know *any* jokes! Ho ho ho! I *love* you, Annie. Here, I'll prove it."

He whipped out a bouquet of flowers and handed it to Raggedy Ann.

"Oh, thank you," she said with a big smile. But as she took the flowers a jet of water squirted all over her. Everybody groaned except the Loonie Knight.

He laughed so hard that tears rolled down his cheeks.

"Now's our chance. Run for it," said Raggedy Andy. "And watch out for the banana peel."

He was too late. The Camel with the Wrinkled Knees skidded and fell, all four wrinkled knees crumpling up beneath him.

"Oh, dear," sighed the Camel with the Wrinkled Knees.

A hole opened up in the forest floor, and all three of them sank down into it.

Dazed, they looked around.

"Look at that great big jukebox!" said Raggedy Ann.

The machine like a jukebox had flashing lights and rolling eyes and it made a funny whirring, clanking sound. But it wasn't a jukebox. Over its huge mouth was a sign that said HA HA HALL.

Suddenly the mouth opened, and out came a long red tongue that looked like a red carpet.

It curled around Raggedy Ann and Raggedy Andy and the Camel with the Wrinkled Knees and lapped them up into its insides. Crazy laughter echoed all around them.

The mouth clanged shut, and suddenly there was silence. In the eerie light there seemed to be no colour except the black and white of the tiled floor.

The three dolls clung to each other, terrified.

Suddenly a loudspeaker zoomed out over their heads, like a living thing.

"Attention—attention, guards!" it boomed. "Three suspicious characters are on the loose. Two rag dolls and a blue camel with wrinkled knees. Don't let them get away!"

The voice echoed and re-echoed, and then there was silence.

Bravely Raggedy Andy stepped forward on to one of the huge tiles, dragging the other dolls with him.

Immediately the tile shot up into the air, sending the three of them flying and falling through empty space.

They landed in water that rushed them headlong through a tunnel and out through a spigot.

"Heh heh heh!"

They could hear the crazy laughter of the Loonie Knight echoing again all around them.

They landed on the rail of a spiral staircase and went sliding down, faster and faster as it curved down, melting into strange loops and whirls, whizzing up and down like a roller coaster, until suddenly there wasn't any rail at all. They were floating in nothingness.

King
Koo Koo

BUMP, BUMPETY-BUMP. Bump, bumpety-bump. That was Raggedy Ann and Raggedy Andy, landing.

THUD. That was the Camel with the Wrinkled Knees.

CLANG. That was the Loonie Knight.

"Oh, it's you again," said Raggedy Ann.

"Sshhh!" said the Loonie Knight.

"Why sshhh?" said the Camel with the Wrinkled Knees, trying to get to his feet.

"Because we're in the Court of King Koo Koo, King of the Loonies," whispered the Loonie Knight.

They came to a stop in front of what looked like an enormous tower.

Two lines of trumpeters appeared, one on each side of the tower. They blew their trumpets very loudly.

The tower started to descend, and the Loonies all around the room chorused, "Hail to our glorious King! Hail to our glorious land! Hail glorious everything, but especially, Hail the King! Heh heh heh!"

When King Koo Koo finally appeared, lowered from the ceiling on a large throne, noisemakers and whistles went off. The room was full of cheers and hoots and yells and crazy laughter from the Loonies.

"Hail to the King!"

Raggedy Ann and Raggedy Andy and the Camel with the Wrinkled Knees stared in amazement. The King of the Loonies was a teeny-tiny fellow, about half the size of Raggedy Ann.

"*That's* glorious?" whispered the Camel with the Wrinkled Knees.

"Sshhh," whispered Raggedy Ann. "Don't be rude." Aloud she said, "Please, Your Highness, you've got to help us. You *are* the King, aren't you?"

The Loonies around the throne tittered and giggled. Some of them looked like circus clowns. Some had rubber noses. Some had accordion necks. Not one of them could keep quiet for a minute.

"Silence!" yelled King Koo Koo.

"Please, Your Highness . . ." began Raggedy Ann.

"You mean Your Lowness, don't you?" snarled King Koo Koo.

"N-no," stuttered Raggedy Ann.

"Yes, you do," said King Koo Koo crossly. "Everybody can see it."

"See what?" said Raggedy Ann, looking down at the angry little King.

"I'M SHORT!" shrieked King Koo Koo.

"You're not *so* short," said Raggedy Ann gently.

"Yes, I am!" screamed King Koo Koo. "I'm just as short as I can be, and everybody knows it. It isn't easy to be big about things when you're small. And anyway, you can never see over people's heads. How can you be boss when you're short? I want to be tall, *tall*, TALL! I want to be the greatest!"

"Maybe you'll grow," said the Camel with the Wrinkled Knees hopefully.

"Besides, it doesn't matter what you look like outside . . ." began Raggedy Ann, but King Koo Koo wasn't listening.

"The only time I can grow is when I laugh at other people," said King Koo Koo.

"That's why I have to bring him people he can laugh at," said the Loonie Knight. "That's why *you're* here. Here, shake hands." He thrust out a hand, and Raggedy Andy politely started to shake it. *Wham*! A boxing glove on a spring hit him in the nose.

"Ha ha, that's very funny!" said King Koo Koo. As he laughed one of his ears started to grow bigger.

When he stopped laughing the ear went back to its tiny size.

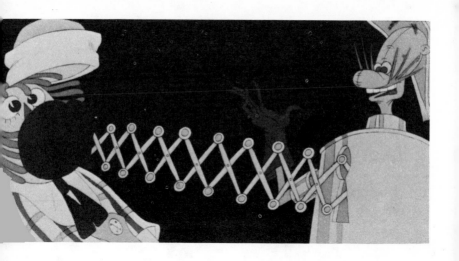

"Did you see that?" whispered the Camel with the Wrinkled Knees.

"Yes," Raggedy Ann whispered back. "I guess that's what he means by having to laugh at other people to grow bigger. Poor thing."

But Raggedy Andy wasn't feeling very kind at that moment.

"Come here and fight, you big tin can," he said to the Loonie Knight.

"No, no, let's be friends," said the Loonie Knight. Again he put out his hand. This time Raggedy Ann stepped forward and took it.

"Ooh!" she cried. A buzzer had gone off and sent a tiny electric shock up her arm.

King Koo Koo jumped up and down on his throne. "Very amusing!" he cried. "I like it." One of his hands grew to enormous size as he laughed.

"Stop that, you bully," Raggedy Andy said to the Loonie Knight.

"Haw haw, better and better," laughed King Koo Koo. Now one of his feet was growing.

"Don't you just love them, Your Majesty?" asked the Loonie Knight, very pleased with himself.

"Yes, yes, they are perfect. They *grow* on me!" He laughed some more at his own joke, and his other foot got bigger.

All the Loonies were cheering and clapping madly. When Raggedy Andy turned to stare at them, the Loonie Knight tickled his neck with a feather.

Surprised, Raggedy Andy jumped about a foot into the air. King Koo Koo laughed so hard his head got to be the size of a balloon.

Raggedy Ann and Raggedy Andy and the Camel with the Wrinkled Knees all stared at King Koo Koo, forgetting to be angry.

"You really do grow bigger when you laugh at other people, don't you?" said Raggedy Andy. "What a way to grow!"

He turned aside in disgust, just in time to get squirted in the face by the Loonie Knight's soda siphon.

"Oh, *very* funny," said King Koo Koo. All of him was now beginning to grow. "If only I could laugh all the time, I'd grow to be the king size I'm meant to be!"

The Loonie Knight suddenly appeared with a whole wagonful of cream pies.

Splot, splot, splot. He threw one at Raggedy Ann, one at Raggedy Andy, one at the Camel with the Wrinkled Knees.

"Delicious," said the Camel with the Wrinkled Knees.

At this King Koo Koo grew to a truly giant size. He was laughing as if he would never stop. And all the Loonies were laughing with him. They started to throw cream pies at one another, giggling hysterically.

One landed on King Koo Koo's face, and he grew so big it seemed he would blow up like a balloon full of air.

An idea began to form in Raggedy Ann's cottony mind. But this was no time to burst any stitches by thinking too hard about balloons.

"Let's get out of here," she said. "*They* are not going to help us find Babette. They're too crazy."

"That's right," said Raggedy Andy. "Let's leave them laughing. Do you see what I see, over there?"

"It's a sign that says N-TRANCE," said Raggedy Ann.

"In this crazy place it probably means WAY OUT," said the Camel with the Wrinkled Knees.

"Right," said Raggedy Andy. "Just what I was thinking. Let's go."

All three of them dropped down on the cream-spattered floor and started inching their way toward the door.

Cream pies were still landing on their backs, but the Loonies were laughing so much they didn't notice that the three dolls had disappeared.

Suddenly King Koo Koo started to grow smaller. And smaller.

"Oh, oh, *ouch*!" he cried. "What's happening? I'm smaller than ever!"

The Loonies, all covered in goo, stopped laughing. Except for a giggle or two here and there, and a yum, yum there and here, there was a terrible silence.

"What have you done, Crackpot?" stormed King Koo Koo. "You have let them escape—the best laughs I ever had!"

The Loonie Knight stood up and looked around in a puzzled way.

"They have gone out through the IN door, you fool," said King Koo Koo. He had sunk way down in his big throne. "But they won't go far," he said after a moment. "Quick, you stupid sardine can, get me my phone. I have an idea."

The Loonie Knight slopped his way as fast as he could through the sea of cream pies. At last he found the telephone and brought it, dripping, to King Koo Koo.

"I will call the Gazooks," said King Koo Koo.

"The Gazooks?" said the Loonie Knight, still giggling feebly.

"Yes," said King Koo Koo. His head grew just a little bigger as he chuckled. "I'm going to have the best laugh of all. It's called the Last Laugh."

He started to push the buttons on the phone with a tiny, gooey finger.

"Hello, that you, Gazooks?"

"Lord of the Deep here," said a watery voice.

"This is King Koo Koo, Gazooks. I have a plan. Now listen carefully . . ."

Captain
Babette

WHEN RAGGEDY ANN and Raggedy Andy and the Camel with the Wrinkled Knees crawled out through the IN door, they had no idea what they would find. Anything would be a relief from all that crazy laughing and pie throwing. But when Raggedy Ann saw what she did see, her smile got bigger than ever. She almost burst a stitch.

"Just what we need!" she said.

What they saw was a boat. A crazy, mixed-up boat, to be sure, with everything from paddle wheels to funnels to an outboard motor, with hundreds of flags flapping in the breeze. Just what you'd expect in Loonieland. But still, it was a boat. Painted in large letters on its side were the words KOO KOO.

"The King's yacht!" cried Raggedy Andy. "Quick, let's hop aboard."

Hop aboard they did, with Raggedy Andy leading the way up the gangplank.

"How do we get this thing going?" he wondered.

"Well, there are two buttons," said Raggedy Ann. "One says STOP and the other says GO."

"I know!" said the Camel with the Wrinkled Knees. "Press the button that says STOP."

"Of course!" said Raggedy Ann. "In this Loonieland, that's sure to make it go."

Raggedy Andy pressed the STOP button, and yes, indeed, the boat took off with a whir and a clank and a blast of its horn.

"Hurray!" cried Raggedy Andy and the Camel with the Wrinkled Knees. "We're off!"

"Yes, but where to?" wondered Raggedy Ann.

She didn't have long to wonder.

"Ship ahoy!" yelled the Camel with the Wrinkled Knees, falling over in his excitement. "It looks like a Pirate boat!"

"It *is* a Pirate boat," said Raggedy Ann. "It's Captain Contagious. Oh, good! Now we can rescue Babette."

"And bring her back to Marcella," said Raggedy Andy happily.

"Yes, and if the Captain will stop being so silly, perhaps we can bring him back, too," said Raggedy Ann.

As they drew nearer to the Pirates' ship Raggedy Andy put the spyglass to his eye.

"Goodness," he said, "they all seem to be having a lovely time on that ship. They are dancing and running around and it looks as if they are singing."

"Probably naughty nautical songs," sighed Raggedy Ann. "The sooner we get Babette off that ship, the better."

And indeed, there was a lot of naughty nautical fun going on aboard the Pirates' ship—for everyone except Captain Contagious and his parrot Queasy.

Babette had been on board only a few moments after the kidnapping from the playroom before she had completely charmed the Pirates. With starry tears brimming from her lovely blue eyes she explained that she was just a poor, homesick little doll who wanted only to return to her home in Paris.

"We will help you!" cried the Pirates.

"No, you won't," said Captain Contagious. "She is my prize, my prisoner. She is mine!"

"Oh, you wicked monster," sobbed Babette.

"Yes, wicked monster," said the Pirates. "Never mind, Babette, we will rescue you. It's a long time since we've had a mutiny."

The wicked Pirates dragged Captain Contagious (and his parrot) down into the deeps of the ship. They locked the Captain in irons, which is what Pirates always do to their prisoners. They even found a tiny pair of chains for Queasy's little feet.

And there the two of them stayed, with only a sputtering candle for light, and only bread and water to feed on.

"Well, at least we have each other," said Captain Contagious gloomily. "Only *you* have remained loyal and true. A-choo!"

"True," echoed the Parrot.

Up on deck the Pirates were having a fine time. They were getting ready to sail for Paris. They were not quite sure where it was, but as long as the beautiful Babette was along, they didn't care.

"Topsail rigged!"

"Mainsail jibbed!"

"Man the pumps and oars!"

"Course set! Sails trimmed and mizzened, Captain Babette!"

"I'm proud of you, my hearty lads!" cried Babette. "We'll sing and dance all the way to Paris!"

74

"Hooray!" yelled the Pirates.

Their boots stamped merrily, their black whiskers waggled, and their noses glowed red with joy.

"My, they certainly are having a good time," said the Camel with the Wrinkled Knees as their ship drew closer.

"Why, Babette doesn't seem to be in any trouble at all," said Raggedy Andy.

"She is, she is," cried Raggedy Ann. "We've got to get her back to Marcella. Can't we make this boat go any faster, Andy?"

"There's no other button to push," said Raggedy Andy.

"What about this thing?" said the Camel with the Wrinkled Knees.

He had found a big lever that said on it, DON'T PULL ME!

"We might as well try it," said Raggedy Ann.

Together they all got hold of the lever.

"One, two, three, PULL!"

The lever pulled clean out of its socket. The three dolls fell flat on their backs.

Bells began to ring. Whistles blew. Sirens went off.

And the ship began to sink.

"Oh, dear," sighed Raggedy Ann. "What have we done *now*?"

"It's all right, Annie," said Raggedy Andy. "Hang on to this thing. You too, Camel."

The "thing" was like a tall, skinny catapult. It stayed above water as the rest of the KOO KOO sank below the waves.

In fact it *was* a catapult.

It took aim and fired. The three dolls went flying through the air.

Bump, bumpety-bump. Bump, bumpety-bump. That

was Raggedy Ann and Raggedy Andy landing on the deck of the Pirate ship.

THUD. That was the Camel with the Wrinkled Knees.

"Again," he groaned, all his legs tangled up.

"What are *you* doing here?" asked Babette in amazement.

"Oh, Babette, thank goodness you're safe," said Raggedy Ann. "We've come to rescue you and take you home with us."

"Rescue me?" said Babette. "And who—or what—is this?" She pointed to the Camel with the Wrinkled Knees.

"This is our new friend, the Camel—"

"—with the Wrinkled Knees," added the Camel, trying to smooth out his wrinkles.

"Hurry and get your things, dear," said Raggedy Ann. "We've got to get back to Marcella's playroom before morning."

"I will not hurry," said Babette. "I will not go anywhere except back to Paris, where I belong."

"Oh," said Raggedy Ann, trying to think. She could feel one of her stitches beginning to burst. "But—where is the Captain?"

"I am the Captain now," said Babette.

"Well, then, where is the Captain, Captain?" asked Raggedy Andy.

"He's down below, in irons, where he deserves to be," said Babette. "Right, me lads?"

"Right, Captain," yelled the Pirates, jumping up and down.

"Seize the prisoners!" cried Captain Babette.

"What are you going to do?" asked Raggedy Andy.

"We are going to hang you from the highest yardarm," said Babette. (She had learned that this is another thing Pirates do to their prisoners.)

"But why?" asked Raggedy Ann, as a wicked Pirate started to tie up her arms.

"So that you will be out of the way until we get to Paris," said Babette.

Raggedy Ann and Raggedy Andy looked at each other. They tried to smile, but inside they were not happy at all.

"Never mind, Andy," said Raggedy Ann. "Never mind, Camel. We've all got each other to love. Nothing can happen to us, as long as we're together."

"I know," said Raggedy Andy, as the rope he was tied to reached the top of the yardarm. "But the terrible thing is, we won't get Babette back to Marcella. Poor Marcella!"

"And I'll never have that home, and all those lovely new friends," sobbed the Camel with the Wrinkled Knees, all four feet tied up. "I knew it—I knew it was too good to be true."

"Don't worry, Camel," said Raggedy Ann. "Something is sure to turn up."

And something did.

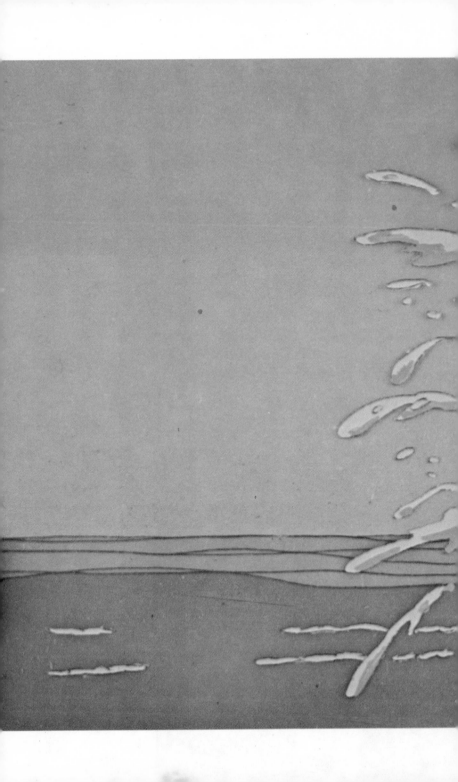

The Gazooks

THE SOMETHING that turned up was King Koo Koo himself. And the Gazooks.

And a more amazing sight you never did see.

The Gazooks, Lord of the Deep, looked like a cross between a sea monster, an old inner tube, and a great green frog. He was distantly related to an octopus. But he had a hundred arms instead of only eight.

At that moment all the arms were whirring and splashing.

"Full speed ahead!" yelled King Koo Koo. He was holding on to one of the arms, swaying and skimming on a pair of water skis. He was very graceful. After all, it is quite easy to be graceful when you are very, very small. Especially when you are a King.

"Why are those little dollies so important to you, King Koo Koo?" gurgled the Gazooks over his shoulder.

"Because they are simple and sweet! They are the nicest people I ever met! And there is no better laugh than laughing at the really good guys. Ha Ha! I feel better already!"

"I see," said the Gazooks, who didn't really see at all. "What is the plan? What are we going to do?"

"We are going to use your talents—all one hundred of them," said King Koo Koo. "You are going to tickle those little dollies until they can't stand it any more. Hee hee! A hundred tickling tentacles going all at once. Can you imagine anything funnier?"

The little King of the Loonies was beginning to grow at the very thought.

"Not boring, not boring at all," chuckled the Gazooks.

King Koo Koo swung in a wide arc on his skis.

"There they are—straight ahead," yelled King Koo Koo. "Get ready to attack!"

Meanwhile, down in the deep, dark hold of the ship, Captain Contagious and Queasy had stopped being sorry for themselves.

Queasy was busy using his sharp little beak on the lock of his irons. In a moment he was free.

"Good work, Queasy. Now mine."

The Captain's irons were bigger and tougher, but at last they fell off with a clang.

"Now let's get up there and take our ship back!" barked the Captain, moustaches twirling again.

Nimbly he climbed the rope ladder and flung open the hatchway.

"What's going on here?" he shouted.

"Help, help, Captain!" called three little voices.

The Captain looked up and saw Raggedy Ann and Raggedy Andy and the Camel with the Wrinkled Knees swinging helplessly from the top of the yardarm.

"Get us down!" called Raggedy Andy.

"Untie 'em, Queasy."

"Aye, aye, Captain," squawked Queasy. He flew up aloft, and in a trice there was a bumpety-bump, bumpety-bump, THUD! and the three dolls landed safely on deck.

"Get back below, you wicked brute," cried Babette. "A-choo! You make me sneeze."

"Can't we be friends, Babette?" asked the Captain. His heart was melting all over again at the sight of the beautiful doll.

But Babette was staring right over his head.

"*Eeeek!*" she screamed. "Look—a sea monster!"

The
Last Laugh

THE GAZOOKS had risen up from the sea, water streaming from his round green face.

King Koo Koo, on water skis, crashed into the side of the Pirate ship.

"Fire one!" screamed King Koo Koo.

A long green tentacle reached out and grabbed the Captain.

"Good," said King Koo Koo, his nose beginning to grow. "Fire two!"

Another tentacle snaked out and got the Camel with the Wrinkled Knees.

"Oh, dear," groaned the Camel with the Wrinkled Knees. "If there's one thing I hate, it's being tickled."

"Hee hee," cried King Koo Koo, beginning to get bigger. "This is the funniest thing I've ever seen. Keep 'em firing, Gazooks!"

The tentacles got Raggedy Andy.

Raggedy Ann grabbed Babette's hand.

"Quick—let's hide in this lifeboat until I think of something to do." She dragged Babette under the tarpaulin cover. Queasy flew in beside them.

King Koo Koo was yelling like the madman that he

was, growing bigger each time a tentacle captured one of the Pirates. Everyone was giggling helplessly, tickled to death.

"Look at me, look at me," shrieked King Koo Koo. "I'm getting bigger and bigger!"

"You see, Babette?" whispered Raggedy Ann. "Marcella told us never to leave the playroom."

"I made a mess of everything," sighed Babette. "What a blow."

"Blow," echoed Queasy.

"Don't let's give up," said Raggedy Ann.

"Up, up," said Queasy.

"What did you say?" said Raggedy Andy as he went whirling past, giggling.

"Blow up," repeated Queasy.

And suddenly Raggedy Ann knew what it was she had been trying to think about. One of her stitches went *pop*.

"Look at the King now," she said. "He's blown up like a balloon. He *is* a balloon! Go and give him a prick, Queasy—he's just full of hot air!"

"Ho ho ho," screamed King Koo Koo. Now he was floating above the ship, an enormous round balloon. Only his head and feet stayed small. "Get the little rag doll! There she is, hiding in the lifeboat."

"This is really great," said the Gazooks, who was enjoying his work. With two tentacles he ripped off the tarpaulin. With another two he grabbed Raggedy Ann and Babette.

"Now tickle them, tickle them!" screamed King Koo Koo. His huge body seemed to fill the entire sky. The galleon looked tiny beneath him.

"Quickly, Queasy," said Raggedy Andy. "Get him!" He gasped for breath, then started to giggle again.

"Oh, wonderful, wonderful," moaned King Koo Koo in ecstasy. "At last I've done it. I've had the Last Laugh. I'm the biggest thing in the world."

He was right, he had had the Last Laugh—*his* last laugh. Queasy streaked up through the air like an arrow. He took aim and dived right into the King's enormous belly.

There was a mighty BANG.

Then there was a great whoosh of air as the balloon-King exploded in a million pieces.

Everybody whirled up into the roaring current of air, holding on to each other, riding on planks, crouching in barrels, clinging to chairs and ropes.

The Gazooks sank with a horrid gurgle.

"Shiver me timbers!" yelled the Captain, moustaches streaming behind him.

"Hang on!" yelled Raggedy Andy, clutching the Camel with the Wrinkled Knees.

"Save me, save me, Raggedy Ann!" screamed Babette.

"Hold on tight!" cried Raggedy Ann.

They all whirled away out of sight and into blackness.

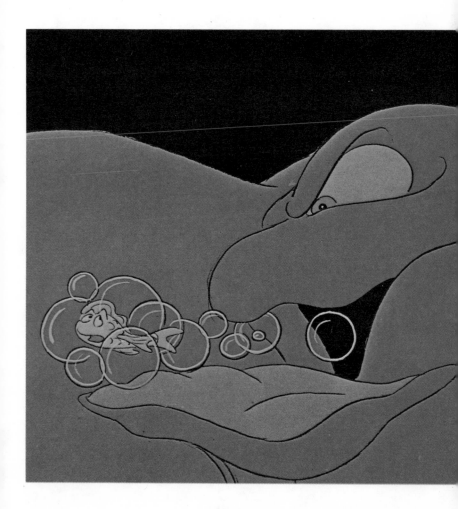

The Camel
Finds a Home

BUMPETY-BUMP, bumpety-bump, THUD.

"Ooh," groaned the Camel with the Wrinkled Knees. "Where are we?"

"Sshhh!" said Raggedy Ann. "We've landed in Marcella's back yard, and here she comes."

The dolls froze where they had landed around the edge of the paddling pool in Marcella's yard.

Marcella came toward them, her red rubber boots squishing in the mud.

"What are you doing out here?" she asked in amazement. "Why, Raggedy Ann, Andy, how did you ever get out here?"

She picked them up and hugged them.

"Oh, Babette, you too! Just look at your lovely dress, all dirty." She picked up the big doll.

"And Captain! What are *you* doing outside of your glass ball?" As she leaned over to pick up the Captain and his ship, she saw a burst balloon and a dirty, greenish inner tube. "Ugh, what horrid things. I wonder how *they* got here."

She carried her armload toward the house, talking softly to them.

The Camel with the Wrinkled Knees stared after them, only his head poking out from the pile of autumn leaves that lay on top of him.

"All alone again," he moaned, as soon as Marcella was out of sight.

Suddenly he heard, or thought he heard, distant music in the sky.

"Wait for me, wait for me!" he called. He struggled to get to his feet, which were more tangled up than ever.

Somehow he managed it, but by that time he couldn't see the camels in the sky anymore. All he could see was the warm light in Marcella's playroom window. Inch by inch he began to climb up the drainpipe that led to the welcoming light. He pressed his nose against the glass, panting.

"Dear Raggedy Ann," Babette was saying. "I am sorry I caused you so much trouble."

"Oh, that's all right, Babette," said Raggedy Ann.

"We certainly did get into a mess or two," muttered Raggedy Andy.

"You are quite right, Andy," said Babette, turning her blue eyes toward him. "I behaved badly."

Raggedy Ann gave her a hug. "Never mind, Babette. It takes a truly wise person to admit being wrong. And to see that simple things are best. You don't need fancy houses or fancy clothes to be happy. Babette, you are one of the bravest people I have ever met."

"I hope you will be my friend," said Babette.

"Of course I will," said Raggedy Ann. "We all will be your friends, won't we, dollies?"

"A-choo!" sneezed the Captain, back on top of the bookshelf. "I'll always love you, Babette."

"You are a very romantic man, Captain," said Babette. "I forgive you for stealing me away."

"Oh, it's so good to be back," sighed Raggedy Ann.

"And it's great to have you back," said all the dolls. "We really missed you."

"Why, look, Andy, there's the Camel!" said Raggedy Ann. "Come on, let's open the window."

All the dolls piled up to help push open the window. The Camel with the Wrinkled Knees tumbled in.

"Everybody!" said Raggedy Ann. "This is our friend, the Camel—"

"—with the Wrinkled Knees," said the Camel, looking shyly down at his tangled-up, saggy-baggy legs.

"He saved our lives and helped us find Babette," said Raggedy Andy.

"And if it's all right with you, I'd like to have him live here with us, so he can have a real home and never be alone again," said Raggedy Ann.

All the dolls crowded around and helped the Camel with the Wrinkled Knees to his feet.

"Of course, of course," said Maxi. "I'll make some new sticks for his legs."

"I'll sew up his patches," said Susan.

"But we like him just the way he is, don't we, Andy?" said Raggedy Ann.

"Any friend of Raggedy Ann's is a friend of ours," said Grandpa. "Isn't that right, everybody?"

"Oh yes, oh yes!" cried the Twin Dolls together.

"Do you really mean it?" said the Camel with the Wrinkled Knees.

"Of course we do, dear, *dear* Camel," said Raggedy Ann. She and Raggedy Andy both put their arms around the Camel with the Wrinkled Knees and hugged him tight. "And we know that Marcella will love you, too."

"Freeze, everybody, here she comes," said Grandpa, who was in charge of looking out.

"Hello, dollies," said Marcella. "What an adventure you must have had! Now I'll have to see about cleaning you up. Why, Raggedy Ann and Andy, who's this?"

Marcella picked up the wrinkled blue Camel.

"Why, it's a darling Camel—with Wrinkled Knees. Welcome to the playroom, Mister Camel." Tenderly she picked him up, stroking his funny, patched humps and feeling his baggy legs. "Somebody must have loved you a lot, once," said Marcella softly. "And now we're going to love you, aren't we, Raggedies?"

She picked up Raggedy Ann and Raggedy Andy and hugged all three of them in her arms. Just for a moment she was almost sure that she heard three happy sighs.

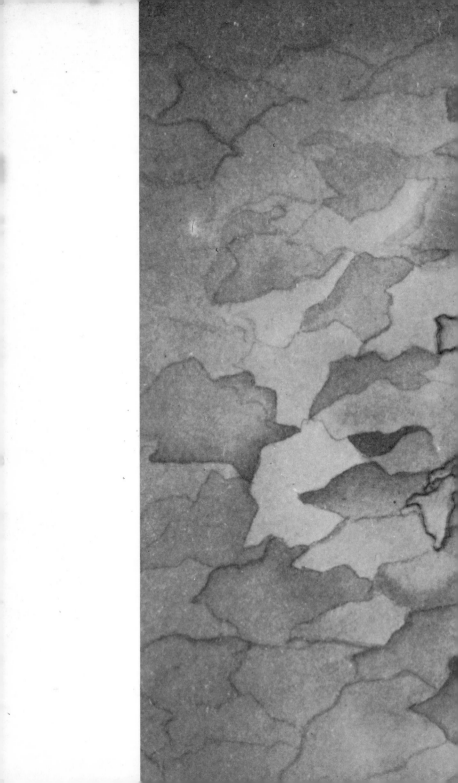

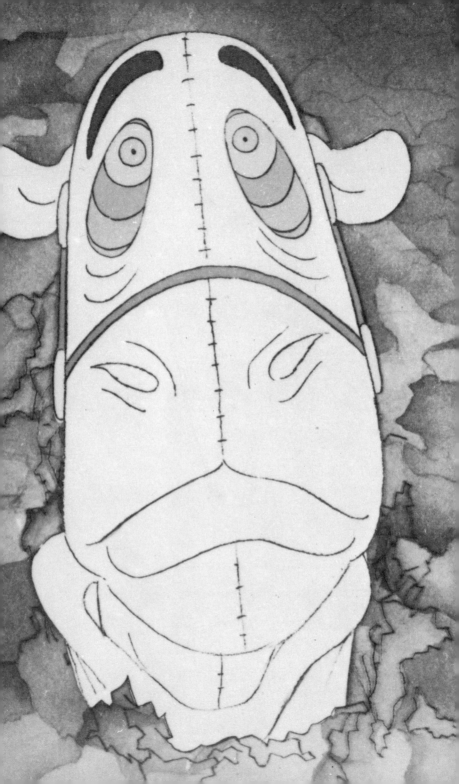